3-D DOT-TO-DOT
SPACE

ARCTURUS

Astronauts

An astronaut is a person trained to travel in space.
The first human to journey into outer space was
Yuri Gagarin, from Russia, who orbited the Earth
in April 1961.

Moon Landings

Lunar modules like this were used to carry astronauts from a spacecraft to the Moon's surface, and back again. The first spacecraft to reach the Moon was Apollo 11 on 20 July 1969.

Planets

Our Solar System has eight planets: Mercury, Venus, Earth, Mars, Jupiter, Saturn, Uranus and Neptune. Saturn is the second largest. It is surrounded by ice crystals that have formed into rings.

Mars Rovers

Machines called rovers have been designed to operate on Mars. They carry several cameras and antennae to help them explore the planet's surface. Then they send information back to scientists on Earth.

Star Gazing

Telescopes magnify faraway objects. They were invented in the Netherlands four hundred years ago. Modern telescopes can be used to see planets, meteor showers, comets and asteroids.

Hubble Space Telescope

This amazing telescope was named after the space scientist Edwin Hubble. It orbits the Earth every 96 minutes, taking wonderful images of distant galaxies and stars.

Satellites

Thousands of man-made satellites orbit the Earth, taking pictures and sending information back to scientists. Satellites help us to predict the weather and to understand the Solar System. They also help our TVs and phones work!

Comets and Asteroids

Comets are made of rock and ice. As they near the Sun, the rock burns and leaves a trail behind it. Asteroids are pieces of rock that orbit the Sun. The biggest asteroid is called Ceres.

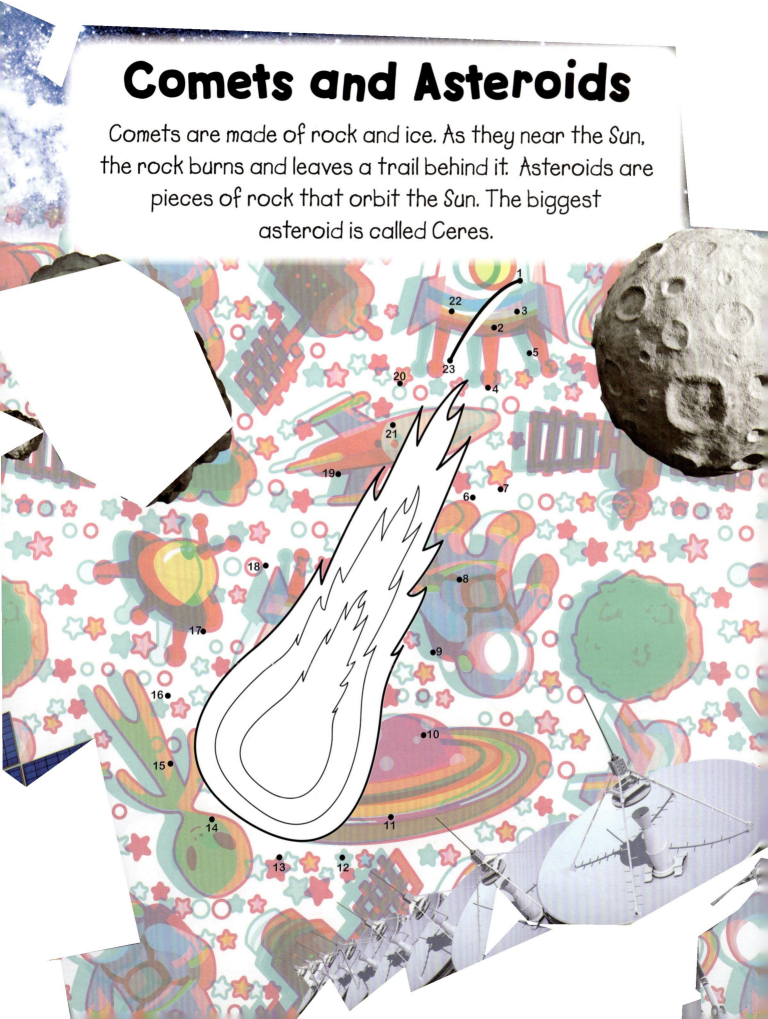

Space Shuttle

Spacecraft are designed to carry people and equipment into space. The Space Shuttle was the first of its kind. It could launch like a rocket, travel through space and land like a plane.

Rockets

3, 2, 1...lift off! A rocket burns huge amounts of fuel to create enough power to blast into outer space. The fuel burns behind the rocket and pushes it upwards.

Aliens

We don't know if space aliens exist although many people claim to have seen them. They are usually described as green beings with large heads and big, oval eyes but they could be any shape or size.

UFOs

This term stands for 'Unidentified Flying Object' and is used to describe alien spaceships. There have been lots of reports of these unusual machines, which are also called flying saucers.

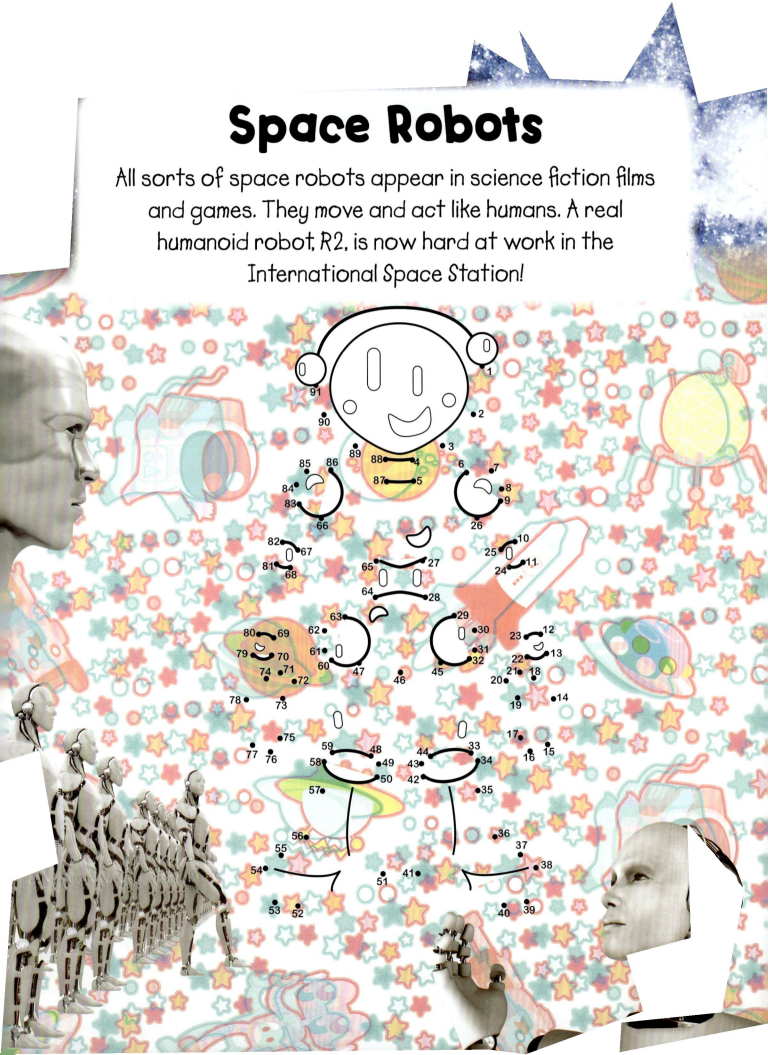

Space Robots

All sorts of space robots appear in science fiction films and games. They move and act like humans. A real humanoid robot, R2, is now hard at work in the International Space Station!

Space Monsters

There are lots of scary space monsters out there with frightening faces, big teeth, huge tentacles and deadly weapons. Luckily, they only exist in books, games and films rather than in outer space... we think!

Space Station

Astronauts can live in a space station for a long time while they carry out research. People have imagined lots of exciting space stations but there are also two real ones in orbit.

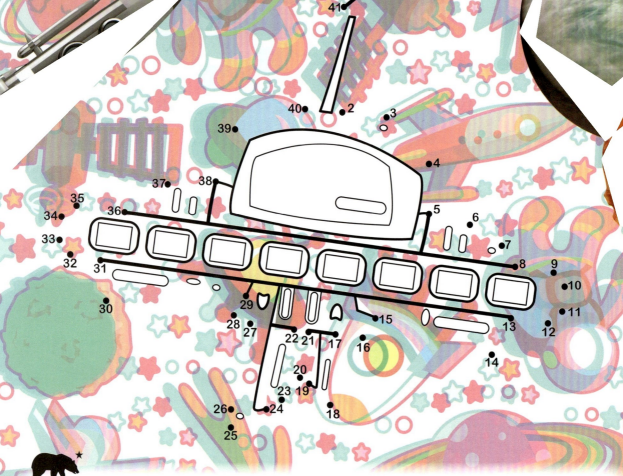

This edition published in 2013 by Arcturus Publishing Limited
26/27 Bickels Yard, 151–153 Bermondsey Street,
London SE1 3HA

Copyright © 2013 Arcturus Publishing Limited

ISBN: 978-1-78212-210-4
CH002731EN
Supplier 01, Date 0313, Print Run 2482
Printed in Malaysia